For Jane, who wears the hats in the relationship. —S. B.

To looking, looking, looking, discovering, and finding. —G. Z.

Library of Congress Cataloging-in-Publication Data available.

ISBN 978-1-4521-8202-5

Manufactured in China.

Design by Jennifer Tolo Pierce.
Typeset in Clifford Pro.
The illustrations in this book were rendered in ink, gouache,
and watercolor paints.

10 9 8 7 6 5 4 3 2 1

Chronicle Books LLC
680 Second Street
San Francisco, California 94107

Chronicle Books—we see things differently. Become part
of our community at www.chroniclekids.com.

The Upside Down Hat

Written by **Stephen Barr**   Illustrated by **Gracey Zhang**

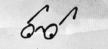

chronicle books · san francisco

One morning, a boy who had everything woke up
and discovered that it was all gone.

Everything was missing

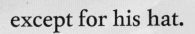

except for his hat.

When it started to storm
he put the hat on

and it kept the rain out of his eyes
while he searched for what he'd lost.

But after a thousand steps
and ten thousand raindrops
he had only his hat
and a terrible thirst.

So he turned the hat upside down

and drank.

When the sun came out

further than it had ever come out before

the boy put the hat back on

and it kept his face from burning

while he searched for what he'd lost.

But after a thousand more steps
and ten thousand beads of sweat
he had only his hat
and a ferocious hunger.

So he turned the hat upside down

and ate.

When the farmer came running up the hill
yelling and spitting about his cherries
the boy put the hat back on
and it kept his face hidden
as he blended into the crowd

and searched for what he'd lost.

He searched for his sewing needle

and his pirate flag

and his bright orange stilts

and his best friends,

Henry and Priscilla,

but after a thousand more steps
and ten thousand strangers
he had only his hat
and a dreadful, helpless feeling.

So he turned the hat upside down

and begged.

All day and all night the boy asked for help
until the streets were empty

and his path was clear.

When the boy made it to the top of the tallest mountain
he looked out over his half of the world
and searched for what he'd lost.

But it was still somewhere else.
And there was nowhere else to go.

So he put the hat back on
because he didn't want to lose
the only thing he had left
while he slept.

And slept.

And slept.

In his dream
the boy was angry
so he turned the mountain upside down

and in the valley it left behind
he found

his sewing needle

and his pirate flag

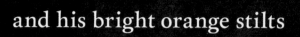and his bright orange stilts

and Henry and Priscilla

and everything else he'd lost,

exactly as he'd left it.

But

his hat was missing.

So he took a few more steps
up and out of the valley

and left everything behind—

until he found his hat
waiting for him.

One morning, a boy who had nothing

woke up

side

       down

and discovered his life was turning around.